THE CONTEMPORARY
ART OF THE NOVELLA

THE CONTEMPORARY ART OF THE NOVELLA

THE UNION JACK

THE UNION JACK

JACK

TRANSLATED BY TIM WILKINSON

MELVILLEHOUSE
BROOKLYN, NEW YORK

THE UNION JACK

FIRST PUBLISHED AS *AZ ANGOL LOBOGÓ*. BUDAPEST :
MAGVETŐ,1995 (ORIGINALLY PUBLISHED 1991)

© 2009 IMRE KERTÉSZ

TRANSLATION © 2009 TIM WILKINSON

FIRST MELVILLE HOUSE PRINTING: NOVEMBER 2009

MELVILLE HOUSE PUBLISHING
145 PLYMOUTH STREET
BROOKLYN, NY 11201

WWW.MHPBOOKS.COM

ISBN: 978-1-933633-87-9

BOOK DESIGN: KELLY BLAIR, BASED ON A SERIES DESIGN
BY DAVID KONOPKA

PRINTED IN THE UNITED STATES OF AMERICA

LIBRARY OF CONGRESS CATALOGING-IN-PUBLICATION DATA

KERTÉSZ, IMRE, 1929-
[ANGOL LOBOGÓ. ENGLISH]
THE UNION JACK / IMRE KERTÉSZ ; TRANSLATION BY TIM
WILKINSON.
    P. CM.
"FIRST PUBLISHED AS AZ ANGOL LOBOGÓ. BUDAPEST : MAGVETOŶ,
1995 (ORIG. PUBL. 1991)"—T.P. VERSO.
ISBN 978-1-933633-87-9
I. WILKINSON, TIM. II. TITLE.
PH3281.K3815A5413 2009
894'.511334—DC22
                2009037830

THE UNION JACK

"fog before us,
fog behind us,
and beneath us
a sunken country"
(Mihály Babits)

If I may perchance wish now, after all, to tell the story of the Union Jack, as I was urged to do at a friendly gathering a few days—or months—ago, then I would have to mention the piece of reading matter which first inculcated in me—let's call it a grudging admiration for the Union Jack; I would have to tell about the books I was reading at the time, about my passion for reading, what nourished it, the vagaries of chance on which it hinged, as indeed does everything else in which, with the passage of time, we discern what, whether it be the consequentiality of destiny or the absurdity of destiny, is in any event our destiny; I would have to tell about when that passion started, and whither it propelled me in the end; in short, I would have to tell almost my entire life story. And since that is impossible, in the lack not just of the requisite time but also of the requisite facts, for who indeed, being in possession of the few misleading facts one deems to know about one's life, could say of himself that he even recognises right away as his life, that process, course and outcome (exit or exitus) which is so totally obscure to himself—himself above all; so probably it would be best if I were to begin the story of the Union Jack with Richard Wagner. And though Richard Wagner, like a persistent leitmotif, would lead us with uncanny sureness, by a direct path, to the Union Jack, I would have to broach Richard Wagner himself at the editorial office. That editorial office exists no more, just as the building in which that one-time editorial office then (three years after the war, to be precise) was for me, for a while, still very much in existence has long existed no more— that one-time editorial office full of gloomy corridors, dusty crannies, tiny, cigarette-smoked rooms lit by bare bulbs, ringing telephones, yells, the quick-fire staccato of typewriters, full of fleeting excitements, abiding qualms, vacillating moods and, later, the fear, unvacillating and ever less vacillating, which seeped out from every cranny, as it were, to squat over every-thing, the one-time editorial office that had long since *not* conjured up long-bygone editorial offices, where in those days I was obliged to turn up at some execra-bly early hour, something like seven o'clock every morning, say. With what sort of hopes, I wonder?—I mused aloud and publicly in the friendly gathering that had been urging me to tell the story of the Union Jack. The young man (he would have been about twenty) who, through a sensory delusion to which we are all prey, I then considered was, and sensed to be, the most personal part of myself, I see today as in a film; and one thing that very likely disposes me to this is that he himself—or I myself—somehow also saw himself (myself) as in a film. This, moreover, is undoubtedly what renders tellable a story that other-wise, like every story, is untellable, or rather not a story at all, and which, were I to tell it in that manner anyway, would probably drive me to tell precisely the opposite of what I ought to tell. That life, that twenty-year-old young man's life, was sustained solely by its *formulability*; that life ground along, with its every nerve-fibre, every fitful effort, solely at the level of *formulability*. That life strove with all its might *to live*, and in that respect stood in contrast, for example, to my present striving, hence also my present formulations, these incessantly miscarried formulations, colliding incessantly against the unformulable, grappling—naturally, to no avail—with the unformulable: no, the striving for formulation, then and there, was actually aimed at keeping the unformulable—namely, the essence, which is to say this life, grinding and stumbling along in the dark, lugging along the burden of darkness—in the shadows, because that young man (I) could only live this life in that way. I engaged with the world through reading, that epidermis around the layers of my existence, as through some form of protective clothing. Tempered by reading, distanced by reading, obliterated by reading, that world was my fallacious but sole liveable, indeed, now and again, almost tolerable world. In the end, the predictable moment arrived when I became a lost cause for that editorial office, and thereby a lost cause for . . . I all but said for society too, had there been a society, or rather if what there was had been a society, then I became a lost cause for what passed for society, for that horde which now whimpered like a whipped dog, now howled like a ravening hyena, always greedy for any provender that it could tear to shreds; I had long been a lost cause for myself, and I almost became a lost cause for life as well. But even at that rock bottom—at least what, at the time, I supposed to be rock bottom, until I got to know depths that were deeper still, ever deeper, depths that were bottomless—even at that rock bottom the formulability was retained, the camera setting, one might say: the camera lens of a pulp thriller, for example. Where I acquired it, what its title was, what it was about, I have no idea. I don't read thrillers any longer, ever since, in the midst of reading one thriller, I suddenly caught myself being utterly uninterested in who the murderer might be; that in this world—a murderous world—it was not only misleading, and actually outrageous, but also quite unnecessary for me to fret about who the murderer was: everybody was. That way of formulating it, however, did not occur to me at the time, some forty years ago, perhaps; it was not a formulation that would have seemed of any use to my strivings at that time, some forty years ago, perhaps, as it was merely a fact, one of those simple—albeit obviously not entirely insignificant—facts among which I lived, among which I had to live (because I wanted to live): it was much more important to me that the main protagonist, a man with an exciting job—a private eye, maybe—had the habit, before embarking on one of his deadly dangerous enterprises, of always "treating himself" to something, a glass of whisky, or occasionally a woman, but sometimes he would make do with an aimless, headlong spin along the highway in his car. That detective novel taught me that a person needs pleasure in those rare intervals in one's torture sessions: until then I would not have dared to formulate that, or if so, then at best as a sin. In those times, deadly dangers were already menacing in the editorial office, deadly boring dangers, to be quite precise, but no less deadly for all that, ever fresher ones every day, albeit the same ones every day. In those times, after a short and utterly inexplicable temporary hiatus, food coupons were again in use, most notably for meat, though quite unnecessarily as it happened—most especially for meat—since there were insufficient meat stocks to justify the reciprocatory gravity of issuing coupons for meat. Around that time, next-door to the editorial office, they opened, or reopened, the so-called Corvin Restaurant, which is to say the so-called Corvin Restaurant in the so-called Corvin Department Store, where (the store being under foreign ownership or, to be more punctilious, in the hands of the occupying power) they even served meat, and without meat coupons at that, although the meat was on offer at double price (in other words, they asked double the price that would have been asked for elsewhere, had meat been on offer anywhere else); and around that time, if the prospect of a fresher, deadly boring deadly danger lay in wait for me at the editorial office, usually in the form of one of those otherwise so splendidly styled "staff conferences," on such occasions I would "treat myself" beforehand to a breaded cutlet in this restaurant (very often out of an advance on my salary for the following month, since the institution of the advance, obviously as the result of some oversight, still remained operative for a while, everything else having long ceased to be operative); and however many and whatever sort of deadly boring dangers to life I might have to confront, the awareness that I had "treated myself" beforehand, the awareness of my foresightedness, my secret, even my *freedom*, that inhered in the couponless breaded cutlet and in the advance on my salary that I had procured to pay for it, about which nobody besides myself could have known, except perhaps the waiter (but then he knew only about the breaded cutlet), and perhaps also the cashier (but then she knew only about the advance)—that helped me through every horror, every ignominy, and every infamy visited on me that

day. For around that time the everydays, the everydays that stretched from dawn to dusk, were transformed into systematic ignominies that stretched
from dawn to dusk, but how they were transformed
into that, the formulation—or series of formulations—
of that otherwise most certainly noteworthy process
no longer figures among the formulations I recollect
now and so, most likely, did not figure amongst my
formulations at the time either. The reason for that,
obviously, may be that my formulations, as I have
already noted, served solely for the rehearsal of my
life, for the bare sustenance of my life that stretched
from dawn till dusk, while they looked on life itself as
a given, like the air in which I am obliged to breathe,
the water in which I am obliged to swim. Quality of
life as an object of formulation was simply left outside
the scope of my formulations, as those formulations
did not serve to gain an understanding of life but, on
the contrary, as I have said, to make life liveable, or in
other words, to avoid any formulation of life. Around
that time, for example, certain trials were grinding
ahead in the country, and to the questions of the
friendly gathering that had been urging me to tell the
story of the Union Jack, the pressing, badgering questions of this gathering, mustered mainly from among

my former students, and so from people mostly twenty to thirty years younger than I, though by that token no longer quite so young themselves, heedless to the fact that with their very questions they were interrupting and distracting me from telling the story of the Union Jack—so to those questions as to whether I had, as it were, "believed" in the counts of the indictments laid out at these trials, whether I had "believed" in the guilt of the accused and so on, I replied that those questions, and most particularly the question of the credibility or incredibility of the trials, did not even cross my mind at the time. In the world that surrounded me then—the world of lies, terror and murder, as I might well classify that world *sub specie aeternitas*, though that does not even begin to touch on the *reality*, the *singularity*, of that world—in that world, then, it never so much as crossed my mind that every single one of those trials might *not* be lies, that the judges, prosecutors, defending counsels, witnesses, indeed the accused themselves, would not all be lying, and that the sole truth which was functioning there, and tirelessly at that, was not the hangman's, and that any other truth would or could function here except the truth of arrest, imprisonment, execution, the shot in the head, and the noose. Only now do I formulate it all so trenchantly, in such decidedly categorical terms—as if then (or even now, for that matter) there had existed (or exists) any solid basis for any sort of categorisation—now that they were urging me to tell the story of the Union Jack, and so I was obliged to tell it all from the viewpoint of a story, to attribute significance to something which has only subsequently acquired significance in the public mind—that bogus awareness raised to the status of generality—but which in the reality of those days, at least as far as I am concerned, had only very slight, or an entirely different, significance. For that reason I cannot assert, for example, that I would have felt morally outraged, say, in connection with the trials that were grinding ahead around that time: I don't recall that I felt that, and I don't even consider it very likely, if only because I did not have a sense of any morality whatsoever—either within me or around me—in the name of which I might have been outraged. But all this, as I say, is to massively overrate and overexplain what those trials meant for me—for a self whom I now see only from a great distance, as on some faded, shaky and brittle film—because in reality they barely grazed my consciousness; they signified, let us say, a gelling of the constant danger, and with that, of course, of my constant disgust, a heightening of a danger that might not yet have been threatening me directly, perhaps, or to express myself poetically, a further darkening of the horizon, in spite of which, however, it was still possible to read, if there happened to be something to read (*Arch of Triumph*, for example). What affected me was not so much the morality of the trials that were grinding ahead then, but rather the influences that ground along at the level of sensibility; hence, the reflexes evoked from me were not moral, but rather those acting at the level of sensory organs and neurological paths—mood reflexes, one might call them, like the aforementioned disgust, then alarm, indignation, fleeting scepticism, general disconcertment and the rest. I recall it being summer at the time, for instance, and that summer had announced itself from the very onset with an almost unbearable heat. I recall that during that unbearably hot summer it had occurred to somebody in the editorial office that the "young colleagues," as it was phrased, ought to partake of some higher, theoretical indoctrination, as it was phrased. I recall that on one especially hot evening of that very hot summer, a bigwig in the editorial office—a Party first-something, a Party bigwig, a bigwig held in general terror, a bigger and more senior bigwig than the senior editor-in-chief himself, though, as far as his authority went, one who was held in a fair degree of hiddenness, if I may be allowed the Heideggerian paraphrase—imparted to us "young colleagues," as it was phrased, this theoretical indoctrination, as it was phrased. I even recall the room in which the lecture was held, the now no longer existing room, the vanished site of which is itself now built over, the so-called "typing pool," by which is to be understood the typewriters, the female typists who operated those typewriters with a furious clatter, the writing desks and ordinary tables, chairs, commotion, countless telephones, countless colleagues, countless sources of sound, all of which, that evening, had already been silenced, removed, tidied away, and transformed into a pious audience, duly seated on the chairs, and the lecturer who was indoctrinating them. I recall that the double-leafed balcony door was wide open, and how much I envied the lecturer for the frequency—by the end, virtually every minute—with which, as if by way of punctuation marks to the lecture, he was able to step outside to cool off on the vast balcony, not stopping until he reached the balustrade, where, leaning out over the parapet, he would look down each time into the

steaming chasm of the Grand Boulevard, and each
time, in the stifling room, I too thought longingly of
the dust-choked, leafy boughs of the roadside trees,
perhaps just stirring in the twilight air, the passers-by
sauntering beneath them, the dilapidated terrace of
the Simplon (later Simpla) Café opposite, the clan-
destine streetgirls clacking by afresh, far from clan-
destinely, on their high-heeled shoes towards their
beats in People's Theatre or Cabdriver Street. It was
all the more conspicuous, though only later did I
attribute any significance to it, that at the end of the
lecture this bigwig, his face boiled red as a lobster,
sweat pouring from his brow, and literally trembling—
from the effort, I supposed at the time (if I supposed
anything at all at the time)—was in no great hurry to
get down to the street; quite the contrary, he was
hardly able to tear himself away from us, addressing
several of us individually, until at long last we were rid
of him, and I too was able to step out onto the balcony
and, with a sigh of relief, look down at the street
where, at that very moment, the bigwig stepped out
of the building and, at that very moment, out of a
black limousine that was idling by the pavement
jumped two ominously helpful men to assist the bigwig most eagerly, but perhaps a touch insistently, into

the black limousine, while in that unexpected hush which sometimes falls for a brief moment, like a climax or an orchestral pause, to interrupt the din of the city in the settling twilight at the end of each unbearable day, the nightmarish lights of the street lamps suddenly lit up. It will come as no surprise to you, mature, cultured people that you are, I said to the friendly gathering, mustered mainly from my former students, which had been continually urging me to tell the story of the Union Jack, to learn where that black limousine took its victim, or that the bigwig had been continually spying down from the balcony on the black limousine waiting below, hoping, for a while, that the black limousine was not waiting for him, then as time passed—during the lecture—slowly ascertaining beyond any doubt that it was indeed for him that the black limousine was waiting, and after that ascertainment all he could do was spin out the time, that is, as far as he was able, delay the moment of departure, the stepping out from the entrance gate of the building; as for me, however, I hardly know what surprised me more, and of course more disagreeably: the encounter four, five or six years later, on what was then still a tree-lined Andrássy (and later Stalin, Hungarian Youth, People's Republic, etc.)

Avenue, with a battered, half-blinded, broken old man, in whom, to my great horror, I recognised the erstwhile bigwig, or the "ad-hoc meeting," as it was called, that was convened in great haste at the editorial office the day following the balcony scene, in the course of which I was obliged to learn certain things, each more absurd than the last, about this bigwig, who just the day before had been a figure of general terror, general homage, general creeping and crawling. These absurdities were brought to our attention now by the hysterically twitching ravings of a pampered youth, now by the incomprehensible outpourings of rage from the senior editor-in-chief himself, a being who, in his mortal terror, had been reduced to some primeval human state, a pulsating amoeba, a mere existential jelly, and had stayed utterly transfixed in that reduced state, yet who only the previous day, scared rigid, had kowtowed and smarmily crept and crawled in the presence of the selfsame bigwig. It would be utterly impossible, and utterly beside the point, for me to recall this man's choice of words, more absurd even than his absurd assertions: they consisted of a farrago of allegations and abuses, protestations, excuses, insults, pledges, threats and suchlike, expressed in the most extreme manner, not eschewing the use of animal names, with the names of canine beasts of prey prominent among the abuses, for instance, and dragging in the language of the most bigoted religious sects amongst the pledges. Now, I would be very curious to know whether the friendly gathering that had been urging me to tell the story of the Union Jack was able, even dimly, to imagine that scene, as I asked them to do at the time, since I myself, sadly, do not possess the requisite powers of evocation or means of expression; however much they may have nodded, strained and tried, I am sure that, in the end, they were incapable of it, simply because it is quite impossible to imagine such a scene. It is impossible to imagine how a grown-up man, well into his forties, who eats with a knife and fork, wears a necktie, speaks the language of the educated middle class and, as senior editor-in-chief, can lay claim to unreserved trust in his faculty of judgement; impossible to imagine how such a man, unless he were drunk or had suddenly gone off his rocker, could all at once wallow in the mire of his own fear and, amid spasms of twitching, squawk streams of such patent nonsense; impossible to imagine such a situation occurring, or rather, since it did occur, impossible to imagine how such a situation could have occurred; and in the end, it is impossible to imagine the situation itself, the scene and all of its details: that group huddled together facing the ranting buffoon, our group of adult men and women in their thirties, forties, fifties, and even sixties and seventies, reporters, stenographers, typists, technicians of every sort, who listened in consternation, with earnest-looking faces and without a single objection, to those near-meaningless ravings that belied all common sense, reason and moderation by their self-negating anger, their veritable paroxysm of self-negation. Let me reiterate: the question of the credibility or incredibility of the words and the accusations—words more fitting to a pulp thriller and accusations reminiscent of mediaeval chronicles of heresy, which went far beyond the orbit of critical judgement—did not so much as cross my mind at the time, for who could have made any judgement there, apart from those who did the judging? What sort of truth would I have been able to perceive there, aside from the truth of that ludicrous and, in essence, childish scene; oh yes, aside from the truth that anybody might be carried off, at any time, in a black limousine, aside from that, in essence, again plain childish, bogeyman-truth? Let me reiterate: the only thing perceived by that stupefied, irresolute, twenty-year-old young man (I), torn between unremitting horror and an unremitting itch to laugh, was that the person who only yesterday had still been a bigwig there was today fit only to be abused with the names of canine predators and to be taken off anywhere, at any time, in a black limousine—in other words, all that he (I) perceived was a lack of permanence. And now, before that friendly gathering which had been urging me to tell the story of the Union Jack, I was unexpectedly moved to declare that maybe morality (in a certain sense) is nothing more than permanence, and maybe people create states which can be designated as lacking in permanence for no other reason than to prevent a state of morality from being established. If this declaration, uttered at the dining table, may of course seem exceptionally slipshod, and probably, indeed in all certainty, untenable under the much more considered circumstances of writing, I still maintain that there does exist at least a close connection between *seriousness* and permanence. For death—if we constantly prepare for it in the course of life as the true, indeed, as a matter of fact, sole task that awaits us; if we rehearse for it, so to speak, in the course of life; if we learn to see it as a solution, an ultimately reassuring, if not satisfying, solution—is a serious matter. But the brick that happens, by chance, to drop right on our head is not serious. The hangman is not serious. And yet, oddly, even someone who has no fear of death fears the hangman. All I intend by all this is to describe, inadequately as it may be, my state, my state as it was then. The fact that, on the one hand, I was afraid, while, on the other, I was laughing, but above all, in some sense, I was confused, or I might even say I reached a crisis point, lost the refuge of my formulations; my life, maybe due to a quickening of tempo or *dynamics*, had become ever more unformulable, hence the sustainability of my way of life ever more questionable. Here I must remind you that professionally I was—or ought to have been—pursuing a formulation of life as a journalist. Granted that for a journalist to demand a formulation of life was a falsehood in its very essence: but then, anyone who lies is ipso facto thinking about the truth, and I would only have been able to lie about life if I had been acquainted, at least in part, with its truth, yet I was not acquainted, either in whole or in part, with the truth, this truth, the truth of this life, the life that I too was living. Little by little, I was therefore recategorised in the editorial office from *talented* journalist to *untalented* journalist. From the moment that I slipped, for a while at least, out of the world of formulability, and thus the sustainability of my way of life, the events going on around me—and hence I myself as an event—disintegrated into fragmentary images and impressions. But the camera lens that captured the jumbled images, sounds and even thoughts was still, agonisingly and irreducibly, *me*, only a me that was growing ever more alienated from myself. The diabolical wooden spoon had once again scraped the very bottom of the human soup in the cauldron of *so-called world history* in which we all stew. I see myself there, in depressed listlessness, at meetings that stretch out to dawn, where the hounds of hell yap, the whip of *criticism* and *self-criticism* cracks on my back, and increasingly I just wait, wait for when and where the door will open through which I shall be ejected who could know where. Before too long I was to be stumbling around in rust-tinted dust beneath the interminable labyrinth of pipes of a murderous factory barrack-complex; bleak dawns smelling of iron castings would await, hazed daytimes when the dull cognitions of the mind would swell and burst like heavy bubbles on the tin-grey surface of a steaming, swirling mass of molten metal. I became a factory worker, but at least it was possible, bit by bit, to formulate that afresh, albeit only with the vocabulary of adventure, absurdity, mockery and fear; that is, with a vocabulary congruent with the world around me, and in that way I more or less regained my life once more. That I might have a chance of regaining life *fully*, indeed that *a full life might be possible at all*—but now that I have already lived this life, now that what still remains of this life (my life) may also be considered as already lived, I must formulate it more precisely, indeed absolutely precisely: that a full life *might have been* possible—that is something I only began to suspect when all at once, after the formulations of adventure, I unexpectedly found myself, dumbfounded and fascinated, face to face with the *adventure of formulation*. This adventure to surpass all my adventures, however, I have to broach, as I remarked in my preamble, with Richard Wagner, but before broaching Richard Wagner, as I have likewise already signalled, I had to start at the editorial office. When they first "took me on" at that editorial office; when I started to go in, day after day, to that editorial office; when, day after day, I telephoned in to that editorial office from the city hall (having been assigned to that column, the "City Hall" column) the latest city hall news, indeed reports, I formulated this aggregation of facts, and not yet entirely without reason, as "I'm a journalist," since appearances, and the activity that engendered those appearances, truly did permit me, by and large, to so formulate it. That was my period of naive formulations, of unbiased formulations, when my way of life and its formulation did not yet stand irreducibly opposed to one another, or in an opposition that was reducible solely by radical means. What had carried me into that career, and therefore into that editorial office, was a formulation, a book I had read, that—above and beyond the necessity of my making a "career choice," so to say, and, yes, above and beyond my irrepressible longing—I might cast off the shackles of parental harassments and a childhood prolonged by education. After stints as a commercial traveller in wines and in building materials had been brought to a close by risible results, indeed quite simply by my having become a laughing stock, then attempts at the printing trade or, to be precise, as a typesetter, had merely introduced me to the experience of futile torment and monotony, quite by chance—if such a thing exists (chance, that is to say), though I personally doubt it—a book came into my hands. This book was a formulation of the life of a journalist, a Budapest journalist who moves about in Budapest coffee-houses, in Budapest editorial offices, in Budapest social circles, pursuing relationships with Budapest women—more particularly, two women, one an aristocratic lady, who was referred to solely by the French brand name of her perfume, the other a girl, a poor, simple, decent creature, palpably finer than the lady of the branded perfume, because she was endowed with spirituality but was born to be oppressed, thereby evoking perpetual twinges of social and metaphysical conscience, so to say—a totally false and falsified formulation, but one that, if memory serves me right, was presented with genuine longing, and thus genuine force of conviction. The book told about a life, a world, that could never have existed in reality, or at best only in formulations, the sort of formulations for which I too was later to strive, for purposes of the sustainability of my way of life, formulations which draw a veil over a life that is unformulable, that grinds ahead in the dark, stumbles about in the dark, lugs the burden of darkness—in other words, over life itself. This book about that journalist, and thus also, to some extent, about journalism itself, held no inkling about journalism in the disaster era, or about disasters at all; the book was *lighthearted* and *wise*, or in other words, an unwitting book, but a book that with the allure of unwittingness exercised a fateful influence on me. The book may well have lied, but, as I recollect, the lying was certainly honest, and it is highly likely that I was in need of just such a lie at the time. A person always lights upon the lie he is in need of just as unerringly and just as unhesitatingly as he can unerringly and unhesitatingly light upon the truth he is in need of, should he feel any need at all of the truth, that is, of liquidating his life. The book presented journalism itself as a sort of happy-go-lucky pursuit, a *matter of talent*, and that accorded fully with the totally absurd and totally unwitting fantasies I spun at that time about leading some sort of happy-go-lucky but still somewhat intellectual life. In some respects I soon forgot about the book but in others, never; I never re-read it, it never again came into my hands, and in the end the book itself went missing somewhere, somehow, and I never looked for it again. Later on, however, as a result of discreetly thorough asking around, I came to realise that the book could have been none other than one of the works of Ernő Szép; more than likely—though this is just an assumption, since I have not corroborated it for myself—his novel *Adam's Apple*. And now that I had mentioned the book that influenced my life so profoundly, with the peculiar determinacy of dreams of a revelatory nature, after some hesitation I also revealed to the friendly gathering where they had been urging me to tell the story of the Union Jack that the author of that book, Ernő Szép, without my being aware that he was the author of the book (by no means one of the most significant of his life's works maybe, if indeed truly significant at all), around that time, that is to say when the disaster had not only long been undeniably visible, present and palpable, but nothing other than the disaster was visible, present and palpable, and, apart from the disaster, nothing else functioned, Ernő Szép was pointed out to me, a so-called "cub reporter," on one or two occasions, in the erstwhile so-called "literary" coffee-houses and cafés which still operated at that time, albeit only as disaster coffee-houses and disaster cafés by then, of course, into which strayed only shadowy figures seeking some warmth, temporary shelter, temporary formulations. And on one or two occasions—perhaps even two or three—I, the "cub reporter," was even introduced to Ernő Szép (who naturally never recalled my earlier introductions), purely for the sake of being able to hear him introduce himself with the phrase that has since attained legendary, nay, mythical status: "I *was* Ernő Szép." At this juncture, I proposed a minute's silence to the friendly gathering of my former students who had been urging me to tell the story of the Union Jack. Because, I told them, as the years and decades pass not only had I not forgotten that form of introduction, it actually came to mind increasingly often. Of course, I said, you would have had to see Ernő Szép, you would have had to see the old chap who, before you would have been able to see him, *was* Ernő Szép: a tiny old chap who seemed to be relieved of his own very weight, swept along the icy streets like a speck of dust by the wind of disaster, drifting from one coffee-house to the next. You would have had to see, I said, his hat, for example, a so-called "Eden" hat, of a shade that had evidently once been what was called "dove grey," which now teetered on his tiny bird's head like a battle-cruiser pummelled by numerous direct hits. You would have had to see his neat, hopeless-grey suit, the trouser legs bagging on to his shoes. Even then I suspected, but now I know for certain, that this introduction, "I *was* Ernő Szép," was not one of those habitual disaster jokes or disaster witticisms of this disaster city which, in the disaster era that had by then undisguisedly set in, were generally believed and accepted, because people could not believe, because they did not know or want to believe or give credence to anything else. No, that introductory form was a formulation, and a radical formulation at that, a heroic feat of formulation, I would say. Through this formulation Ernő Szép remained, indeed became the essence of, Ernő Szép, and at the very time when he already only *was* Ernő Szép; when they had already wound up, liquidated and taken into state ownership every possibility by which Ernő Szép had once still been permitted to be Ernő Szép. Simply a lapidary formulation of the actual truth condition (the disaster), couched in four words, which no longer had anything to do with wisdom or lightheartedness. A formulation which lures nobody towards anything but with which nobody can ever be reconciled, and by that token a formulation with a far-reaching resonance—indeed, in its own way, a creation which, I will hazard a guess, may survive all of Ernő Szép's literary creations. At this, my friends and former students started to mutter, some of them sceptically objecting that anyway the oeuvre was, so to say, "irreplaceable," as they put it, and moreover Ernő Szép is at this very time gaining a new lease on life, at this very time people are starting to re-read and re-evaluate his works. I knew nothing, and in this instance once again don't even want to know anything, about this, since I am not a literary man; indeed, for a long time now I have not liked, and do not even read, any literature. If I search for formulations, then I usually search for them outside literature; if I were to strive for formulations, I would probably refrain from formulations that are literary formulations, because—and maybe it suffices to leave it at this; indeed, there is truly nothing more that I can say— literature has fallen under suspicion. It is to be feared that formulations that have been steeped in the solvent of literature never again win back their density and lifelikeness. One should strive for formulations that totally encapsulate the experience of life (that is to say, the disaster); formulations that assist one to die and yet still bequeath something to posterity. I don't mind if literature, too, is capable of such formulations, but what I see increasingly is that only *bearing witness* is able to do this, possibly a life passed in muteness without being formulated *as a formulation*. "For this cause came I into the world, that I should bear witness unto the truth"—is that literature? "I *was* Ernő Szép"—is that literature? Therefore—and only now do I notice it—the story of my encounter with the adventure of formulation (and at the same time with the Union Jack) does not start, as I originally supposed, with Richard Wagner after all, but with Ernő

Szép; in either case, however, one way or the other, I have to and had to start with the editorial office. In the editorial office to which my fantasy, under the influence of Ernő Szép, had borne me—under external circumstances ready, as ever, to comply with steadfast fantasy—in that editorial office, then, on a briefer and more condensed trajectory, so to say, though of course without leaving behind an intellectual trail of any kind, I trod the very same path that Ernő Szép had taken, from the unwittingness of wisdom and lightheartedness up to the "I *was* Ernő Szép" type of formulation; all that I found on the site of the alleged erstwhile Budapest was a city that had tumbled into ruins, lives that had tumbled into ruins, souls that had been tipped into ruins, and hopes trampled underfoot amid those ruins. The young man about whom I am speaking here—I—was also one of those souls, stumbling around on the way to nothingness amid those ruins, although he (I) at the time still construed the ruins merely as some kind of film set and himself as an actor in a film—in any event, some splenetic, some acerbically modern film that was fraudulent in an acerbic and modern manner—a role that, being based entirely on the illusion seen from the auditorium, and oblivious to all disturbing circumstances (that is to say, reality, or the disaster), he (I) formulated as "I'm a journalist." I can see the young man on drizzly autumn mornings, the fog of which he inhaled just like the rapidly evaporating freedom; around him I can see the set, the blackly glistening wet asphalt, the accustomed bends in familiar streets, their dilatations into the void over which the swirls of thinning fog gave hints of the river; the dank smell of the people who waited with him for the bus, the wet umbrellas, the hoarding plastered with garish posters which concealed the wartime rubble of a ruined building, on a site where today, forty years later, another ruin stands, a peacetime ruin, the wartime ruined building having been replaced by a peacetime ruined building, a decrepit, eight-storey monument to total peace, corroded by premature death, patinated by air pollution, vandalised by every sort of squalor, theft, neglect, infinite provisionality and futureless indifference. I can see the stairway up whose stairs he will hurry before too long, with the same sense of security that delusion-driven people have which had impelled him (me) to declare "I'm a journalist"—with a certain sense of self-importance, in other words, which even the stairway in itself nurtured, that already long non-existing stairway, which hinted at a then unambiguous reality, the reality of *real* editorial offices, *late* journalists, *one-time* journalism, and the mood and reality which embraced all this; I can see the lame porter, the so-called "errand-boy" or, more accurately, office messenger, that singularly priceless person, who in those days was still so singularly priceless merely due to the singularly priceless services he rendered, limping nimbly between the rooms of the editorial office as he fetched and carried manuscripts and galley-proofs and performed trivial but indispensable errands as zealously as he was ready to act as a lender of last resort for cash loans (at low interest), if the worst came to the worst; a person who only later on turned into an all-powerful, implacable, unapproachable Office Assistant, wrapped in the pelt of his arrogance, of the sort familiar to us solely from Kafka's novels and, to be sure, so-called *socialist reality*. On one such early-autumn morning, no, it was more likely forenoon already, most probably around the time of the gradual decrescendo from the clamorous chords of going to press, the "deadline," in those languid moments of slackness deriving from a certain sense of what could be called satisfaction, it happened that one of the stenographers in the editorial office raised with me the question of which theatre I wanted free tickets for. The stenographer—I still remember him today: his name was Schaeffer, and although he was at least fifty years older than I was, I, like everyone else, called him Wee Schaeffer, since he was a diminutive, exquisitely dapper little chap, with his neat suits, fastidious neckties, French-style footwear, one of those cast-off *parliamentary stenographers* consigned to oblivion in an era when Parliament had long ceased to be a parliament, and stenography was no longer stenography in an era of ready-made texts, off-the-peg texts, prefabricated, pre-digested and meticulously censored disaster texts—this stenographer, then, with his rounded little eunuch's paunch, his bald egg-head, his face reminiscent of carefully ripened soft cheeses, his little eyes shifting anxiously in their narrow slits, therefore required especially tactful handling, all the more so as he was hard of hearing, something of a paradox, to put it mildly, for a stenographer, and as such—when in prisons and diverse penal institutions in the selfsame city, indeed just a few blocks away, the numbers of people standing in corridors, hands behind their backs, faces turned to the wall, were already starting to multiply rapidly, when summary courts were churning out their sentences at full blast, when everybody outside prison walls, everybody indiscriminately, could be regarded only as a prisoner released on indefinite parole—he continually fretted that his deafness, which everyone knew about, might accidentally be exposed and he might be sent into retirement: this stenographer, then, was the one who used to keep a record of the claims and entitlements to free tickets of the so-called colleagues in that editorial office. I can still remember the ambivalent surprise that caught the young man, whom, as I say, I sustained and felt myself to be at the time, in the wake of the stenographer's accosting me at all, for on the one hand, he (I) had no heart for going to the theatre, simply on account of the disheartening plays that were being performed in the theatres, while on the other hand, he was entitled to regard the mere fact of being accosted as marking the end of his apprenticeship, his coming of age as a journalist, so to speak, since free tickets were earmarked exclusively for fully qualified and paid-up so-called colleagues. I remember that we perused the miserable options for a while with honest, one might say fellow-suffering scepticism—he, an old man simplified to his trivial practical fears, and I, a young man with more complex and more general anxieties—during which our gazes, so foreign and yet so intimate, communed for a few seconds. There was one other choice: the Opera House. "*Die Walküre* is on," he said.

At that time I did not know the opera. I knew nothing at all about Richard Wagner. All in all, I knew nothing about any operas, had no liking for opera at all, though as to why not, that would be worth reflecting on, but not here, not now, when I really ought to be telling the story of the Union Jack. Suffice it to say that my family liked opera, which may make it somewhat easier to understand why I didn't like opera. What my family liked, though, was certainly not the operas of Richard Wagner but Italian opera, the pinnacle of my family's taste, I almost said tolerance, being the opera *Aida*. I grew up in a musical milieu—insofar as I can call my childhood milieu a musical milieu at all, which I cannot, because I would call my childhood milieu any other milieu but a musical milieu—where the remarks that were passed about Richard Wagner, for example, were of the kind "Wagner is *loud*, Wagner is *difficult*" or, to mention a remark made in connection with another composer, "If it has to be a Strauss, then make it Johann," and so forth. In short, I grew up in a milieu that was just as stodgy in respect to music as it was in every other respect, which did not leave my taste completely unscathed. I would not venture to state categorically that it was exclusively the influence of my family, but it is an indisputable fact that, up until the moment when I got my ticket to Richard

Wagner's opera *Die Walküre* from the stenographer Schaeffer in that editorial office, I liked instrumental music exclusively, and I disliked any music in which there is singing (excepting the *Ninth Symphony*, and by that I mean Beethoven's, not the Mahler *Ninth Symphony*, which I got to know later on, much later on, at just the right time, at a time when thoughts about death were manifesting, when I was making acquaintance with thoughts about death, indeed, what I would have to call a process of familiarising myself with, if not exactly befriending, thoughts about death), as if in the human voice alone, or to be more precise, the singing voice, I saw some kind of polluting matter which casts a poor light on the music. All the musical precursors of which I partook prior to hearing the Wagner opera had been purely instrumental precursors, chiefly orchestral, which I got to at best sporadically, primarily through the agency of that exceedingly testy old man at the Music Academy, known to every student or student type, who, due to some eye defect, wore a perennial look of distrust but, for a forint or two pressed into his palm, would let any student or student type into the auditorium, testily ordering them to stand by the wall and then, as soon as the conductor appeared at the stage door leading to the podium, would direct them in a harsh voice to any unoccupied free seats. It would be fruitless for me to muse now over why, how, and on what impulse I came to like music; it is a fact, however, that around that time, when I was still not yet able to call myself a journalist, when my perpetually problematic life was perhaps at its most problematic because that life was at the mercy of my family, a family that was already on the point of breaking up around that time, and subsequently, during the disaster era, broke up completely, to be dispersed into prisons, foreign countries, death, poverty, or even, in the rarer cases, prosperity, a life from which already then, as ever since, I was constantly obliged to flee; it is a fact, therefore, that even then, as little more than a child, I would have been unable to tolerate that life, my life, without music. I think it was that life which prepared me, or in truth I should say rather that life which *rehearsed* me, for the disaster-era life which ensued not long afterwards, palliated as it was by reading and music, a life comprising several separate lives that played into one another's hands, each one able to annihilate the others at will, yet each holding the others in balance and constantly offering formulations. In this sole respect, purely in respect of this balancing, the balancing of small weights, my seeing and hearing *Die Walküre*, being receptive to *Die Walküre*, being overwhelmed by *Die Walküre*, undoubtedly represented a threat in a certain sense: it cast too big a weight onto the scales. What is more, that event—Richard Wagner's opera *Die Walküre*—had an impact like a street mugging, a sudden attack for which I was unprepared in every sense. Naturally, I was not so uninformed as to be unaware that Richard Wagner himself had written the librettos of his operas, making it advisable to read through the texts before listening to his operas. But I was unable to procure the libretto for *Die Walküre*, any more than Wagner's other librettos, a state of affairs to which pessimism induced by my milieu, and lassitude induced by that pessimism—a lassitude that was always instantly ready for renunciation of any kind— no doubt also contributed, though to be completely fair I should add that in the disaster era, which happened to be the era in which Richard Wagner began to interest me, Richard Wagner was actually classified as an undesirable composer, and thus his opera librettos were not available for sale, his operas were generally not performed, so to this day I don't understand and don't know why *Die Walküre*, of all his operas, was being performed, and with a fair degree of regularity at that. I do recall that some sort of so-called programme booklet was on sale, the sort of disaster-era programme booklet which, alongside (disastrous) synopses of other operas, ballets, plays, marionette shows and films, also provided a five- or six-line synopsis of the "content," so to speak, of *Die Walküre*, out of which I understood nothing at all and which presumably—though this did not occur to me at the time—had been deliberately contrived in such a way that nobody should understand it; in truth, to hold nothing back, I was even unaware that *Die Walküre* was the second piece in an interlinked tetralogy. That was how I took my seat in the auditorium at the Opera House, which even in the disaster era was still an exceedingly agreeable, indeed splendid, place. What happened to me is what came next: " . . . the lights in the auditorium went down and below their box the orchestra broke into the wild pulsating notes of the prelude. Storm, storm . . . Night and tempest . . . Storm, a raging tempest, in the forest. The angry God's command resounded, once, twice repeated in its wrath, obediently the thunder crashed. The curtains whisked open as though blown by the storm. There was the rude hall, dark save for a glow on the pagan hearth. In the centre towered up the trunk of the ash tree. Siegmund, a rosy-cheeked man with a straw-coloured beard, appeared in the timber-framed doorway and, beaten and harried, he leaned against the door-post. His sturdy legs, wrapped round with hide and thongs, carried him forwards with tragically dragging steps. Beneath his blond brows and the blond forelocks of his wig his blue eyes fixed the conductor with an imploring gaze. At last the orchestra gave way to the tenor's voice, which rang clear and true, though he tried to make it sound like a gasp . . . A minute passed, filled with the singing, eloquent flow of the music, rolling its waves at the feet of the events on the stage . . . Sieglinde entered from the left . . . They looked at each other with the beginning of enchantment, a first dim recognition, standing rapt while the orchestra interpreted in a melody of profound enchantment . . . Again their glances met and mingled, while below the melody voiced their yearning." Yes, that is how it was. Try as I might to follow it, straining my ears and eyes to the utmost, I understood not a single word of the text. I had no idea who Siegmund and Sieglinde were, who Wotan and the Valkyrie were, or what motivated them. "His wrath roared itself out, by degrees grew gentle and dispersed into a mild melancholy, on which note it ended. A noble prospect opened out, the scene was pervaded with epic and religious splendour. Brünnhilde slept. The God mounted the rocks." Yes, whereas I stepped out of the Opera House onto Stalin Avenue, as it happened to be called at that time. I shall not attempt—naturally, it would be pointless to do so—to analyse right here and now the so-called *artistic impact* or *artistic experience*; in essence—to resort, against my better judgement, to a literary simile—I walked in much the same way as the main protagonists in *Tristan und Isolde* (another opera by the same composer, Richard Wagner, which at that time I knew about only by hearsay) go around after they have imbibed the magic potion: the poison had penetrated deep within me, permeated me through and through. From then onwards, whenever *Die Walküre* was performed, as far as possible I would always be seated there, in the auditorium, for the only other refuge that I found where I might occasionally shelter myself, if only with an all-too-fragile fugacity, during that period of general, which is to say both public and private, disaster, apart from the auditorium of the Opera House and the, sadly, all-too-sporadic performances of *Die Walküre*, being the Lukács Baths. In those two places, immersed in the pure sensuality of the then still green, hot-spring water of the Lukács Baths and in the both sensually *and* intellectually very different ambience of the ruddy gloom at the Opera, every now and then, in lucky moments, I would become aware of a presentiment, unattainably remote of course, of the notion of a private life. Even if such a presentiment, as I have already mentioned, was fraught with a certain implicit danger, I could not help sensing its *irrevocability*, and I was able to place my trust in that solid sentiment as in a kind of *metaphysical solace*: put simply, even in the lowest depths of disaster, and in the lowest depths of consciousness of that disaster, I was never again able to carry on living as if I had not seen and heard Richard Wagner's opera *Die Walküre*, as if Richard Wagner had not written his opera *Die Walküre*, as if that opera and the world of that opera did not subsist as a world in the disaster world. That was the world I loved; the other I had to endure. Wotan interested me; my editor-in-chief did not. The enigma of Siegmund and Sieglinde interested me; that of the world which was really around me—the real disaster world—did not. It goes without saying that I was unable to formulate all this for myself so simply at the time, since it was not, nor could it be, so simple. I suppose that I conceded too much to the terror of so-called reality, which thereafter appeared to be the inexorable reality of the disaster, the one and only, unappealable, real world; and although for my own part, I was now—after *Die Walküre*, through *Die Walküre*—*unappealably* aware of the reality of the other world as well, knowing of it, as it were, only in secret, in some sense with an illicit and thus incontrovertible but nevertheless guilty knowledge. I suppose I did not yet know that this secret and guilty knowledge was in fact a *knowledge of myself*. I did not know that existence always sends word of itself in the form of secret and guilty knowledge, and that the world of the disaster was in fact a world of this secret and guilty knowledge raised to the point of self-denial, a world which rewards only the virtue of self-denial, which finds salvation solely in self-denial, and which is therefore—however we look at it—in some sense religious. Thus I saw no *connection* of any kind between the disaster world of *Die Walküre* and the real disaster world, even though, on the other hand, I had unappealable cognisances of the reality of both worlds. I simply did not know how to bridge the chasm, or rather, to be more accurate, schizophrenia, which separated these two worlds, just as I did not even know why I should feel it was my task—and a somewhat obscure, somewhat painful, yet also somewhat hopeful task at that—to bridge that chasm or rather, to be more accurate, schizophrenia. " . . . He looked down into the orchestra pit. The sunken space stood out bright against the darkness of the auditorium and was a hive of industry: hands fingered, arms drew the bows, cheeks puffed out, humble—all these assiduous mortals laboured zealously to bring to utterance the work of a master who suffered and created; created the noble and simple visions enacted above on the stage above . . . Creation! How did one create? Pain gnawed and burned in his breast, a drawing anguish which was yet somehow sweet, a yearning—whither? for what? It was all so vague, so shamefully unclear. Two thoughts, two words he had: creation, passion. His temples glowed and throbbed, and it came to him as in a yearning vision that creation was born of passion and was reshaped anew as passion. He saw the pale, spent woman hanging on the breast of the fugitive man, he saw her love and distress, and he knew: so life must be to be creative"—I read those words like somebody who was reading for the first time in his life, like somebody who was encountering words for the first time in his life, secret words that spoke to him alone, interpretable by him alone, the same thing as had happened to me when I saw *Die Walküre* for the first time in my life. The book—Thomas Mann's *The Blood of the Walsungs*—was about

Die Walküre, as its very title divulged. I began reading it in the hope that I might learn something about *Die Walküre* from it, and I put the book down in a shock of amazement, as if I had learnt something about myself, as if I had read a prophecy. It all fitted: *Die Walküre*, the fugitive existence, the distraughtness—everything. I ought to note here that between first receiving *Die Walküre*, my first engulfment by *Die Walküre*, and my first engulfment by this little book, years— suffice to say, years full of vicissitudes—had passed; so, in order to clarify my assertion that "it all fitted," I shall be obliged at this point to digress slightly, to give at least an outline of the circumstances in which I was living at the time, all the more so that I too may find a steady bearing in the weft of time and events and not find I have lost the thread of this story, the story of the Union Jack. This book—*The Blood of the Walsungs*—came into my hands after my wife-to-be and I, with the assistance of a good friend of ours, one fine summer morning traversed half the city, from the former Lónyay, then Szamuely and today once again Lónyay, Street with a four-wheeled tow cart on which were piled, to put it simply, the appurtenances of our rudimentary household. This happened in the nick of time, since the lodgings in Lónyay (or Szamuely)

Street that my wife-to-be and I had been inhabiting had by then started to become unbearable and uninhabitable. I had become acquainted with my wife-to-be in the late summer the year before, just after she had got out of the internment camp where she had been imprisoned for a year for the usual reasons—that is to say, no reason at all. At that time, my wife-to-be was living in the kitchen of a woman friend from earlier days, where the woman friend had taken her in—for the time being—because somebody else happened to be living in my wife-to-be's apartment. That somebody else, a woman (Mrs Solymosi), had taken over the apartment under extremely suspicious—or if you prefer, extremely usual—circumstances immediately after my wife-to-be's arrest, through the intervention of exactly the same authorities who—essentially without any verifiable reason, indeed on no pretext at all—had arrested my wife-to-be. Practically the moment she learned of my wife-to-be's release, that somebody else (Mrs Solymosi) immediately requested my wife-to-be (by registered letter) to instantly have the furniture my wife-to-be had unlawfully stored in the apartment that rightfully belonged to *her* (Mrs Solymosi) removed to the place where they were currently lodged (which is to say, the kitchen of the woman friend from earlier days who was taking her in for the time being). When later, thanks to a protracted legal action, but above all let us just say to unpredictable circumstances—let's call it a stroke of luck—my wife-to-be got her own apartment back, we discovered, among some abandoned odds and ends, books, and other junk, pegged together with a paper clip, a bundle of paper slips covered with the pearly letters of a woman's handwriting, from which I don't mind quoting a few details here, under the title of, let's say, "Notes for a denunciation" or "Fragments of a denunciation," purely as a contribution to a legal case-study or even to an aesthetics of the disaster, as follows: "She has lodged various complaints against me at the Council and the police, that I illegally moved into the apartment and stole hers . . . She imagined she could scare me with her slanders and I would give up the apartment to her . . . The apartment has been allocated definitively; there is no space for her furniture in my apartment . . . *Furniture*: 3 large wardrobes, 1 corner couch, 4 chairs . . . She should put them into storage, I am under no obligation to keep them after what is already 1½ years . . ." There follow a few items of data that would appear to be reminders: "17/10/1952 application, 29/10 allocation, 23/11 apartment opened up, inventory taken,

15/11 move in, 18/11 ÁVH [State Security], Council =
ÁVH, ÁVH 2x—no response, Rákosi's secretariat . . .
In September of 1953 Mrs V. [i.e. my wife-to-be] Mrs
V. a.m. . . . Asked her by reg. letter to remove furn . . .
Have to keep my own furniture in cellar because I'm
looking after her stuff . . . Her wardrobes are crammed
full of dirty clothes, under ÁVH seal, they can't be
aired . . . She claims she doesn't have an apartment
and is staying as a guest with somebody. Does that
mean she doesn't need the things in the wardrobe?
The woman puts on a good act and is quite capable of
sobbing, if required, but I've had enough of that and
I won't tolerate her furniture in my apartment any
longer—." So we had had to spend the disaster winter
that lay before us, which was ushered in at the very
start by temperatures of twenty to twenty-five degrees
below zero, in various temporary shelters, including
the aforementioned kitchen of the woman friend
from earlier days, a spare room of distant relatives sur-
rendered on a very explicitly temporary basis, an
exceptionally charmless sublet room, made especially
memorable by its ice-cold latrine on the outside cor-
ridor, and so on, until a miracle—admittedly, all too
temporary as it turned out—in the shape of Bessie, a
former snake charmer and her Lónyay (or Szamuely)
Street sublet apartment, dropped into our lap. It

doesn't matter in the slightest now how and why this miracle occurred, although it would be wrong to leave out of this story—the story of the Union Jack—the earthly mediator of this heavenly miracle: a grey-templed gentleman, known as Uncle Bandi Faragó in the cafés and nightclubs around Nagymező Street, who, somewhat flashily for those times—the disaster time—and the occasion—the disaster—used to dress in an aristocratic green hunting-hat, a short sheepskin coat and English-style tweeds, whose face glowed with a permanent suntan even in the deathly pale winter, and besides that allegedly pursued the exclusive occupation of a professional conman and adulterer, as was indeed confirmed decades later when, from a newspaper bought out of sheer absent-mindedness (since the so-called news was of no real interest), I was silently and genuinely shocked to learn about his death in a well-known common prison, where, allegedly, a permanent cell, his slippers and a bathrobe were set aside for him even during the days that he spent on release; and who one afternoon, in one of those cafés around Nagymező Street, one of those cheap, noisy, draughty, gloomy and filthy cafés with music which, since the state, though holding them to be iniquitous, at least heated well and kept open until late at night, had become an illicit day-and-night shelter for outcasts and in which my wife-to-be and I were, so to say, temporarily residing much of the time instead of in our temporary residences, suddenly came up to our table, and, really without any prior or more direct introduction, declared, "I hear you're looking for lodgings, my lad." Then to my apathetic admission, which ruled out all hope in advance: "But why, dear boy, didn't you come to *me*?" he asked in a tone of such self-explanatory, such deep and uncomprehending reproach that, in my shame, I was lost for words. Later, after we had gone to the imparted address in Szamuely Street, where the door was opened by a lady, getting on in years and—as Gyula Krúdy might have put it—of statuesque figure, with yellow forecurls peeking from under her green turban, the face slightly stiffened by heavy makeup, and wearing a curious silk pantaloon besprinkled with magical stars and geometrical designs, who, not content with a verbal reference, did not allow so much as a toe into the hallway until she had glimpsed the message written in Uncle Bandi Faragó's own hand on Uncle Bandi Faragó's own calling card; so when this lady led us, my wife-to-be and me, to the room that was to let, a spacious corner room with a bay window, the dominant furnishings of which were a decidedly oversized divan big enough for at least four persons, a mirror placed in front of it, and a standard lamp with a shade plastered with all sorts of obsolete bank notes (including the million- and billion-pengő denominations that had been in currency not so long before) that gave a mystic lighting effect, my wife-to-be and I did not doubt for one second the original purpose to which the room had been put, and it seemed most probable (and at once a clue to the miracle) that around that time, in that era of denunciations, the room's intended purpose—who knows, perhaps due to a denunciation that just happened to be pending— did not, all of a sudden, to be concise, seem expedient. Things may have changed by the spring, but during that winter we had the chance to peek into our landlady's past: we could see her as a young woman, wearing an ostrich-plumed silk turban, with a giant speckled snake coiled around her naked back, in some nightclub in Oran, Algiers or Tangiers, which there, in that Lónyay (i.e. Szamuely) Street disaster-sublease, struck one as indeed quite extraordinarily implausible, and we could handle and ritually marvel at a profusion of relics which were every bit as implausible; later on, however, the snake charmer became despondent, and it was apparent from her increasingly consistent demeanour that, above and beyond the hostile feelings towards people that naturally arise in one as time goes by, she was not guided so much by the random targets of that transcendental antipathy as by palpably down-to-earth goals: she wanted to regain her room, because she had other, presumably more lucrative, plans for it. I shall try to skip the details as rapidly as possible, for I can only relate those details in this spirit, the spirit of formulability, which is by no means the same thing, of course, as the real spirit of those details, which is to say the way in which I lived and survived that reality; and this nicely illustrates the iron curtain that rises between formulation and being, the iron curtain that rises between the storyteller and his audience, the iron curtain that rises between one person and another, and, in the end, the impenetrable iron curtain that rises between a person and himself, between a person and his own life. I woke up to all this when I read those words: " . . . he saw her love and distress, and he knew: so life must be to be creative." Those words, all at once, awakened me to my life; all at once, I glimpsed my life in the light of those words; those words, or so I felt, changed my life. That book which, from one second to the next, swept away the haze of my formulations from the surface of my life, so I might see that life, all at once, face to face, in the fresh, startling and bold colours of seriousness, I discovered in the new (that is, repossessed) apartment—absolutely out of place, absolutely implausibly, in the manner, as I remain convinced to this day, of a miracle that spoke to me alone—among the forgotten odds and ends, the above-mentioned denunciation slips and, thumbed to tatters, several volumes of pulp, shock-worker, partisan and romantic novels, the latter of defunct imprints. That book, so I felt, marked the start of the radicalisation of my life, when my way of life and its formulation would no longer be able to stand in any sort of contradiction with one another. By then, the time when I had been a journalist, or even a factory worker, had already long gone; by then I had committed myself to my seemingly boundless, but also supposedly boundless and intentionally boundless studies, being able, thanks to a congenital ailment, to absent myself from my occasional jobs for months on end without running any immediate risk in the meantime that my mode of existence would, in all likelihood, qualify as a crime of so-called "publicly dangerous work-shyness." At that time all this completely preoccupied me, producing in me a sense of exaltation, of *mission.* I suppose it was then that I became acquainted with the experience of *reading*, *reading* for nothing in particular, an experience in no way comparable with the experience of reading as it is generally understood and designated, the sort of reading bouts, or mania for reading, which might overcome a person at best just once or twice in a lifetime. Around that time there also appeared a book by the author of *The Blood of the Walsungs*, a volume of essays, in which there was an essay on Goethe and Tolstoy, whose chapter titles alone—"Questions of Rank," "Illness," "Freedom and Eminence," "*Noblesse Oblige*," and the rest—were enough in themselves almost to dumbfound me. I recall that I read this book all the time and everywhere I went; the essay on Goethe and Tolstoy was tucked under my arm all the time and everywhere I went: it was with me when I boarded trams, went into shops, wandered about the streets—and so also, one especially fine early afternoon in late autumn, when I set off for the *Istituto Italiano di Cultura per l'Ungheria*, the Italian Institute of Culture, where at the time, in my boundless thirst for knowledge, I was learning Italian, and during my passage across the city I registered, indeed, here and there, even participated, at least as an astounded spectator, in the intoxicating events of a day that was later to become memorable, a day that I or anybody else could hardly have guessed would turn into that particular memorable day. I was, I recollect, somewhat surprised when I turned off Múzeum Boulevard into the otherwise normally deserted Bródy Sándor Street, hurrying towards the nearby palace of the Italian Institute, which had originally been built as the one-time Hungarian Parliament. The lesson, however, started at the normal time. After a while, the street noise penetrated into the room even through the closed window. Signore Perselli, the finicky, jet-black-moustached *direttore*, for whom, on his rare visits to lessons, it took no more than a blatantly clumsy pronunciation of the word *molto* to be excited into demonstrating how it should be done with Italian fluidity, with the initial "*o*" closed and the final "*o*" short, the intervening consonants being articulated with the tongue drawn back, almost like saying "m*a*lto," on this occasion burst into the room in genuinely frantic haste to exchange a few no doubt diplomatically apprehensive words with our teacher before scurrying on to the other classrooms. A minute later, everybody was at one of the windows. In the slowly gathering dusk I could clearly see that on the left, towards the front, green rockets were being launched from the Hungarian Radio building above the heads of the darkly milling crowd of protesters there. At that very moment, from the opposite direction, three open-topped trucks turned into the street out of Múzeum Boulevard; from above, I had a good view of the militiamen with the green markings of border guards who were seated on the benches, rifles squeezed between their knees. On the back of the first truck, leaning against the driver's cabin, stood a lieutenant, evidently the commander. The crowd fell quiet, opened ranks, then roared. It is quite unnecessary here for me to evoke the manifestly pathetically affecting words that they started to shout to the soldiers down below, words which only at that given moment, that elevated moment of pathos, were able to exert an effect of genuine pathos. The trucks slowed down in the dense crowd, then came to a halt. The lieutenant turned about and raised an arm aloft. The last of the trucks now started to back out of the street, to be followed by the other two, amidst jubilation from the crowd. At this moment, we who, from an Italian diplomatic viewpoint which held itself to be above and beyond all this, had no doubt suddenly become unwelcome guests, capable of who knew what sort of emotional or other manifestations, were ordered to gather downstairs, beneath the long, neo-

Renaissance vaulting of the entrance. The heavy, two-leafed gate was bolted from the inside with iron bands. There we squashed together, between the sounds assailing us from outside and the security guards standing by behind us, until the Institute's burly porter, evidently on some signal, swung the iron bands back and swiftly threw open the gate though which each and every one of the sixty to eighty of us, on a vigorous shove being applied from the rear, found ourselves, in a trice, deposited outside on the by now twilit street, in a vortex of buffeting sound, swirling movement, ungovernable passions and inscrutable events that teemed between the buildings. In the ensuing days, my attention was divided between the essay on Goethe and Tolstoy and the events that raged outside; or, to be more precise, the cryptic and unformulable promise that inhered in the essay on Goethe and Tolstoy, in the gradual comprehension and eventual acceptance of it, was linked in my mind, in a strange but quite self-explanatory manner, with the equally unformulable, similarly uncertain but, at the same time, wider-ranging promise inherent in the external events. I cannot say that the events that were stirring externally diminished my interest in the essay on Goethe and Tolstoy: to the contrary, they height-

68

IMRE KERTÉSZ

ened it; on the other hand, I also cannot say that while I was totally immersed in the world of the essay on Goethe and Tolstoy and the spiritual and intellectual jolts of that experience, I *also* absent-mindedly paid occasional attention to the events that were stirring in the street: no, that is not what happened at all; I would have to say instead, however strange it may sound, that the events stirring in the street *vindicated* the heightened attention paid to the essay on Goethe and Tolstoy; the events stirring in the street during those days thereby *bestowed a genuine and incontrovertible sense on the heightened attention I was paying to the essay on Goethe and Tolstoy.* The weather turned autumnal; several quieter days ensued; down below on the street, of course, but especially on looking out from the window, I could see how much the street had changed: detached overhead tramway cables snaking between the rails, dangling bullet-riddled signboards, smashed windows here and there, fresh holes in the peeling stucco of the houses, dense throngs of people on the pavements of the long, long street, all the way up to the distant corner, and very occasionally a vehicle, a passenger car or lorry, tearing by at great speed, with some highly conspicuous distinguishing marks, the more garish the better. A hurtling jeep-like vehicle suddenly appeared, with the British red-white-and-blue colours, a Union Jack, draped over the entire radiator. It was scudding at breakneck speed between the crowds thronging the pavement on either side when, sporadically at first but then ever more continuously, evidently as a mark of their affection, people began to applaud. I was able to see the vehicle, once it had sped past me, only from the rear, and at the very moment when the applause seemed to coalesce, almost solidify, an arm stretched out hesitantly, almost reluctantly at first, from the left-side window of the car. The hand was tucked into a light-coloured glove, and though I did not see it close up, I presume it was a kid glove; probably in response to the clapping, it cautiously dipped several times parallel to the direction in which the vehicle was travelling. It was a wave, a friendly, welcoming, perhaps slightly consolatory gesture which, at the very least, adumbrated an unreserved endorsement and, by the by, also the solid consciousness that before long that same gloved hand would be touching the rail of the steps leading down from an aircraft onto the runway on arrival home in that distant island country. After that, vehicle, hand and Union Jack—all disappeared in the bend of the road, and the applause gradually died away.

So much, then, for the story of the Union Jack.

"Johnny rejoiced wholeheartedly in the prospect of the fight—I think that neither he nor Brattström would have shared my apprehensions," I read during the severe winter that soon set in, during which my aforementioned ailment flared up again, so to speak, in the form of a fever of reading, or perhaps it was my reading fever which flared up again not long afterwards in the form of the aforementioned ailment. "Johnny repeatedly assured me, with the delightful rolling of his r's, that the two boys were in deadly earnest and certainly meant business. Complacently and with a rather sardonic objectivity, he weighed the chances of victory for each . . . He gave me my first impression of the peculiar superiority, so typical of the English character, which later on I came so greatly to admire," I read.

What naturally also belongs to the story, perhaps needless to say, is that several days later, on that same bend in the road, but coming from exactly the opposite direction to that in which the Union Jack had disappeared, tanks suddenly veered into sight. All but wavering in their haste, their uneasiness, their fear, they always paused for a moment at that bend. And though the road, the pavement, the district, the city, everything was by now wholly deserted, with not a person, not a sound, not a soul to be found anywhere, the tanks, as if anticipating even a stray embryonic thought, each and every time let off a single cannon round, strictly one, before clattering onwards. Since the gun position, direction, and trajectory were always the same, for days on end they always pounded the same first-floor windows, outside and eventually interior walls of the same decrepit, Secessionist-style apartment block, so that finally the yawning void looked for all the world like a corpse's mouth, gaping in terminal wonderment, all of whose teeth were about to be knocked out one by one.

But here we really do reach the end of the story of the Union Jack, this sad but maybe not all that significant story. It would never have entered my head to tell it had that friendly gathering of former students, mustered to celebrate, there's no denying it, my all-too-round-numbered birthday, not appealed to my better nature, while my wife was busy in the kitchen preparing a cold snack and drinks for them. For them, they said, for "younger people," there are no longer any, as they put it, "primal experiences," they only ever know and hear about tales of heroism and horror stories, or perhaps horrific tales of heroism and heroic horror stories . . . that birthdays are a fine thing but, with due consideration to my fluctuating blood pres-

72

IMRE KERTÉSZ

sure, my "revolutionary" pulse of at best forty-eight beats per minute, the pacemaker that I will anyway, sooner or later, find is unavoidable . . . not to put too fine a point on it, lest I too should take my stories and experiences, my whole knowledge of life, with me to the grave, when there are hardly any more authentic witnesses and tellable tales, and that they—a "generation," as they put it—are left here with their wealth of objective but totally lifeless and routine knowledge and facts . . . and so forth. I tried to reassure them that there was nothing wrong about this; that, anecdotes apart, every story and everybody's story is one and the same story when it comes down to the essentials, and that these essentially selfsame stories are really essentially all horror stories; that essentially every event is really a horror event, and even history too had long, long ago become, essentially, at best just horror history. But then how was it, they asked at this point, that in the course of my own particular horror history I was able to recount spiritual and intellectual experiences of the kind that I had recounted; what had become of the continuation of what, in the course of my account, I had called "my mission"; or had I, perhaps, given up on the "mission"; moreover, what had stood out for them from my entire story was something, they said, that they had actually always suspected and assumed about me, namely, that by retreating inconspicuously into my own narrow area of expertise, I had lived a diminished life though I might also have pursued an intellectual existence and, if merely in my area of expertise, been creative—in other words, as they said, where and how had the "break" in my, so to say, "career" occurred. I was staggered to hear this, for it meant I had told them the story of the Union Jack to absolutely no purpose; it seems that they, children of destruction, no longer understand, are *unable* to understand, that the devastation of total war was turned by total peace into complete and, so to say, perfect destruction. Just one remark about an intellectual existence: even if I had happened to pursue an intellectual existence, I could only have done this at the price of self-denial; that is, I could only have pursued at best the *appearance* of an intellectual existence; thus, whether I chose an intellectual existence or I chose to forsake an intellectual existence, in any event self-denial had been the one and only choice open to me. And so, reckoning that naturally they would anyway not understand, were *unable* to understand, I tried to explain to them that it was not at all a matter of my, as it were, "relinquishing" what I had characterised as my mission, which is to say that there should no longer be a contradiction between my way of life and its formulation, or at least not a radical contradiction. I cited that great philosopher of history, Wilhelm Dilthey, with whom I had endeavoured—so far as I could, so far as I was *free* to do so—to familiarise them, my former students, when they were still in their student years: "Understanding presupposes living, and an event only becomes a life experience if understanding guides living out of its narrow and subjective being into the realm of the whole and the general." I, so I feel, had done that. I had understood that I could only be creative here in the act of self-denial; that the sole creation possible in this world, *as it is here*, is *self-denial as creation*. I may have expressed myself extremely, but that doesn't matter, since they didn't understand anyway: to that extent, and in consistent cognisance of that, I told them, I had lived, understood, and fulfilled, if I may put it this way, the morally obligatory experience of life—life *as it is here*, and to that extent my life is a life of paying witness—so I am content. I reminded them of the formulations cited in the story, the story of the Union Jack: "For this cause came I into the world, that I should bear witness unto the truth," and

"I *was* Ernő Szép." There is no more ultimate lesson, no more complete experience, than those. As to what this is all for, what *precisely* this is for, what experience is for—that's another question, I reflected later. Who sees through us? Living, I reflected, is done as a favour to God. And whilst attention turned to the arrival of the dishes, the glasses raised and clinked in celebration of my birthday, I reflected, if not exactly with impatience but with a certain sense of expectant relief, that the more promising future which is nowadays threatened from all sides is something that I myself neither have to live through nor understand.